For Henry

—R. M.

For Franz

—C. S.

The Big Ball of String

Ross Mueller · Craig Smith

ALLEN&UNWIN

George wanted to play soccer.
But he didn't have a soccer ball to kick.
All he had was a big ball of string.

George decided he could use his big ball of string for a game of soccer.

But his mum said he couldn't kick his ball in the house because he might break something important.

So . . . George decided he should go to the park.

He carried his ball of string out of the house and past the milk bar,

past the postbox and around the corner. Past the fire station . . .

. . . and into the park where the magpies were warbling.

He put his ball of string down on the ground
and he began to play soccer.

He kicked it and he kicked it and he kick, kick, kicked it!

George kicked the ball all over the park!

He kicked it and he kicked it and he kick, kick, kicked it!

The ball rolled and the ball bounced!

He kicked it and he kicked it and he kick, kick, kicked it! Back past the fire station and around the corner.

MILK

He kicked it and he kicked it and he kick, kick, kicked it!

Past the postbox and past the milk bar …

and soon George found himself back at his house.

But the ball of string had disappeared.

George could not see it anywhere, no matter how hard he looked.

Maybe the ball of string was back at the park.

So George walked out of his house, past the milk bar,
past the postbox and the fire station and into the park.

And just near the tree
where the magpies were warbling,

he saw a piece of string.

George decided to roll up the string and see what was at the other end.

He rolled it and he rolled it and he roll, roll, rolled it.

George rolled up the string all over the park!

He rolled it

and he rolled it

and he roll, roll, rolled it!

He **rolled** it as fast and as tight as he could.

He rolled it and he **rolled** it and he roll, roll, **rolled** it!

Back past the fire station, around the corner, past the postbox and past the milk bar.

He rolled it and he rolled it and he roll, roll, rolled it!

And soon he was back at his house.

George looked down and there in his hands was

the big ball of string.

George wanted to play soccer again.

So he kicked it and he kicked it
and he kick, kick, kicked it . . .
he kicked his ball of string

all the way back to the park.